ISBN-13: 978-1508740308
ISBN-10: 1508740305

Book Website
www.nadinepoper.weebly.com
www.meilidesigns.com

Printed in U.S.A

Holly, Dolly, and Molly are three dachshunds who love wearing proper dog attire. Then there is their friend Farfel. An enjoyable story told in rhyme about friendship and standing up for yourself. Will Farfel gather the confidence to be her own dog?

Wienies in Bikinis

by Nadine Poper

Illustrated by Kaitlyn and Jessica Reber

To mom and Rachel~N.P.
To our family~K.R. and J.R.

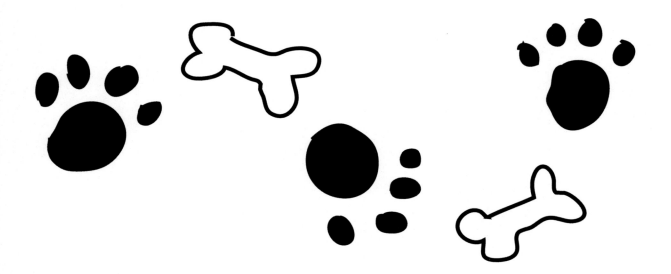

Holly

Dolly

Molly

Farfel

Holly's sweater is purple.
Molly's sweater is pink.
Dolly wears a sweater in different shades of ink.

Farfel's sweater is . . . well, isn't. You see,
Farfel likes to wear bikinis but . . .

...wienies don't wear bikinis!

Holly's dress is lacy.
Molly's dress is frilly.
Dolly wears dresses that are
just so silly.

. . . wienies don't wear bikinis!

Their costumes come in all shapes and sizes. Dolly's costume even won prizes.

Farfel's costume didn't win. She never entered in because...

...wienies don't wear bikinis!

Dachshunds in moccasins,

but no wienies in bikinis!

OMG! Collars jewel-studded

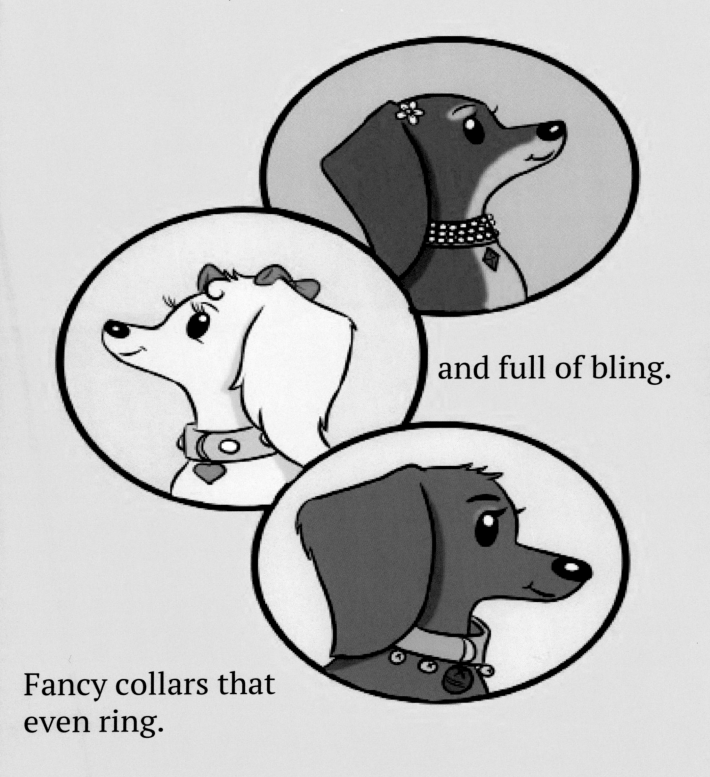

and full of bling.

Fancy collars that
even ring.

Wear collars AND swimwear...What?? No way! "Swimwear only," Farfel will say.

At bedtime

jammies are cozy and soft.

They are perfect for dozing off.

PJ's for Farfel cannot be found.
PJ's make her frown BIG time!

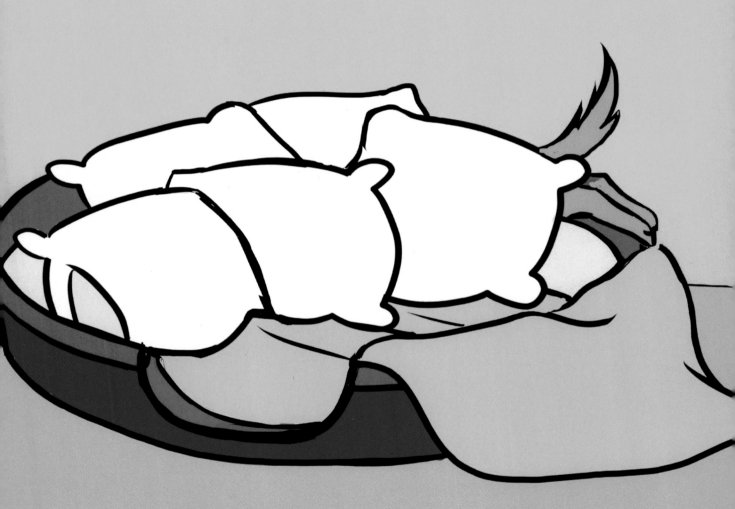

So . . .

. . .what is Farfel
going to do?

"A hoodie won't do. It's not who I am.

Please understand. I am me and you are you."

This is what I am going to do.

Wienies DO wear bikinis!